I0609983

John Rowell Waller

Unstrung Links

John Rowell Waller

Unstrung Links

ISBN/EAN: 9783337333959

Printed in Europe, USA, Canada, Australia, Japan

Cover: Foto ©Andreas Hilbeck / pixelio.de

More available books at **www.hansebooks.com**

UNSTRUNG LINKS:

DROPPED FROM THE DISJOINTED CHAIN OF A TOILING LIFE,
AS THE RINGING CHORUS OF NATURE'S MUSIC BEAT TIME ON
THE ANVIL OF A RESPONDING HEART:

BY

JOHN ROWELL WALLER.

Aid the dawning, tongue and pen;
Aid it, hopes of honest men;
Aid it, paper—aid it, type—
Aid it, for the hour is ripe;
And our earnest must not slacken
     Into play.
Men of thought and men of action
     Clear the way!
            CHARLES MACKAY.

DARLINGTON:
WILLIAM DRESSER, 41, HIGH ROW,
1878.

PREFACE.

SINCE the author of this work has taken the liberty to appoint me to introduce his volume of "Unstrung Links" to the world, I will certainly take the liberty to do it in my own way. I feel no hesitation in recommending the work to the perusal of all readers of taste. The author is a true poet, and whoever reads his works cannot help but come to this conclusion. He is only twenty-three years of age, yet, judging by his works, you would really suppose that he must at least be forty. His poems are the production of an ingenious mind, more matured than you would think possible in a man so young. He is not unknown in the world of letters; thousands will remember *John Rowell Waller*, *Lucy Vane*, or *Rolan Wall*, at the end of sweet lyrics which have appeared in almost every paper and periodical in the North of England again and again for a length of time. Those sweet, touching, harmonious pieces were always welcome, because they spoke to the heart, and found an echo in every true, manly, and womanly breast. Poetry, like music, painting, or sculpture, when it is truly good, you feel it to be so: there is something in your souls which accords with it, and you are convinced that it is the genuine article—no need of any recommendation from others. I am but a poor panegyrist, but I will venture to predict that this work, after being read, will give rise to far higher enconiums than mine. These "Unstrung Links," I fancy, are destined to form a chain which will hereafter bind the listening and enchanted world to the tuneful and soul-stirring author.

Secure the work, ladies and gentlemen! Read it! and it must succeed.

R. ABBOT.

CONTENTS.

— — —

UNSTRUNG LINKS.

THE LITTLE GRAVE UNDER THE SNOW.

There's a neat little grave in our snug churchyard,
   Concealed 'neath a mantle of snow,
Close down by the side of the rustic porch
   Where in summer the daisies grow ;
In the waning light of an afternoon,
   A Sabbath not long ago,
They buried her deep in the cold, cold earth,
   In that little grave under the snow.

Escaping the cares of the after-life,
   The struggles, and sorrows, and tears,
The rumble and din of contending strife,
   And the buffets of after years ;
Free from all these in the sheltering earth,
   Till the trumpet of summons shall blow,
Free from the trials that follow our birth,
   In the little grave under the snow.

True ! there's a father on earth, whose love
    Its object will certainly miss ;
But there is a Father who watches above
    To guide her through realms of bliss ;
The spirit is with its compassionate God,
    And the angelic face is aglow
As she watches the body beneath the green sod,
    In that little grave under the snow.

Ah ! doubtless, she looks from the land of blue,
    And watches her mother in tears,
And watches the children who miss her, too,
    And she'll watch in the coming years ;
Watching for ever the home of the dead,
    In the toiling world below,
Where the leaves from the bending trees are spread
    O'er that little grave under the snow.

And the Spring will come with its primrose tints,
    And the Summer with violets sweet,
And the Autumn, aroma'd in mellowing light,
    Will follow in gold-clad feet ;
And Winter again with his evenings long
    O'er the sleeper will rudely blow,
And the robin will twitter the old, old song,
    Near the little grave under the snow.

And the father will sit by the lonely hearth,
  And think of his poor dead dove,
Whose soul from the body is parted and gone
  To sit 'mong the angels above ;
And the children, at times, as they wander to church,
  A look of mute sorrow will throw
At that mound of earth near the rustic porch—
  The little grave under the snow.

LOST !

November's chill, wild, moaning blast,
  Went howling through each leafless tree,
And o'er the earth he ruthless cast
  The leaves, in wild terrific glee ;
The leaden clouds of threat'ning size,
Loomed darkly in the wintry skies,

And o'er the drear and lonesome moor,
  A weary traveller bent his way,
From storm and wind quite insecure,
  No house or shed before him lay ;
Against the wind he hurried on,
The rain drops pattered one by one.

A soldier was he, and a man
　　Who, from the battle-field unharmed
Had breasted death, and now began
　　To feel uneasy and alarmed ;
The rain came faster to the ground,
The thunder roared and burst around.

At intervals the lightning flashed,
　　And bright the moorlands shone upon,
And then again the thunder crashed,
　　And still the wanderer struggled on ;
Struggling to reach his friends and home,
Never again from them to roam.

Outworn and faint he battled still,
　　Weary and cold and quite unmanned ;
Nature gave way despite his will,
　　Until he could no longer stand,
From home and friends full many a mile,
He sank, a cold and lifeless pile.

And he, who braved the battle's din,
　　Lay stretched upon the lonely wild ;
His soul to Heaven was gathered in
　　Beside the Shepherd-Saviour mild ;
A traveller there next morning led,
Found, and sent home the soldier, dead.

THE SOLDIER'S OAK.*

Full fifty summers' suns have fled
   Upon the dreary past,
Since, stretched upon a humble bed
   A warrior breathed his last.

Ah ! 'twas a sad and solemn sight—
   The spirit cased in clay,
Burst from the darkness into light,
   And sped to realms of day.

In days gone by his youthful heart
   Had panted with delight,
At thought that he might act a part
   In fierce and deadly fight.

For there are men whose hearts seem tuned
   To music of the wars,
Whose souls repeat in harmony
   The thunder-songs of Mars.

* The incident on which the above verses are written,
is mentioned in "Chambers's Journal," among other burial
eccentricities.

I've 'erewhile marked some youthful face,
    With dark and flashing eye,
And supple limbs, and noble grace,
    And forehead fair and high,

With close-set lips that plainly told
    The youth for soldier framed ;
The future man of sterling gold,
    Whose soul should ne'er be tamed.

And he was such an one, who lay
    In life's last solemn stage,
In whose last thoughts some dreamings may
    Have been of battle's rage.

For in his youth he ever thought
    Of scenes on field and flood,
As oft he read of conflicts fought
    For home and country's good ;

How men had braved the din of strife
    In hardy days gone by,
How heroes bold had yielded life
    And died in victory.

And ever, as he thought and read
    Of men of gory fame,
He shed warm tears for noble dead,
    And longed to do the same.

And every day would bring new life
　　To prompt his wild desire
To shed his blood in battle's strife,
　　Amid the hottest fire.

And growing as his years grew on,
　　From youth to man's estate,
The sea of strife he launched upon,
　　And left the rest to fate.

And when in peace, in barrack laid,
　　He chafed at indolence,
Till news of war's exertion made
　　His heart sweet recompense.

Then, when the gathered storm had broke,
　　And battle raged and boomed,
His form showed first among the smoke,
　　Where danger thickest loomed.

With white steel drawn he trod the field
　　Unbending and erect ;
And no foe's frown could make him yield,
　　And naught his progress check'd.

In hottest fire he ever fought,
　　And none his heart could tame,
Till up to glory's height he wrought,
　　And there engraved his name.

And over on the old home shore
 A loved one nightly knelt,
And to earth's God sweet spirits bore
 The prayers she breathed and felt.

And anon, as the glorious news
 Of vict'ry reached her ears,
She breathed her thanks to missioned winds
 That bore them up the spheres.

And holding firm her baby boy,
 She thought of days to come ;
And told her heart of floods of joy,
 When *he* should reach his home.

But ah ! a messenger of doom
 Sped from the death-fraught line,
And his life's sun went down in gloom
 When most it seemed to shine.

Awhile in pain he lingered on ;
 The summons came at last ;
The soul his comrades loved was gone,
 And o'er the bourne he passed.

But ere the final stroke was given,
 That soothed his troubled breast,
He held a comrade's hand, and made
 A serious last request.

" When I am dead, my body take
　Away to my dear home,
And in some open pasture make
　In England's soil a tomb.

" No coffin shall enclose my bones,
　But in the fertile earth
Lay me," he said in solemn tones,
　" Near where I had my birth.

" And over me plant acorns deep,
　And let them shoot and grow ;
Then that which is the strongest keep
　To bloom while years shall go.

" For though I've lived for naught but strife
　Now that my power is broke,
My bones shall nourish up to life
　A sturdy British oak."

Then, with a last farewell to all,
　Of home and friends he sigh'd :
He breathed the names of those he loved,
　Then closed his eyes and died.

As was his will they took him home.
　And as he'd wished, they did ;.
For in a solitary tomb
　The hero's bones they hid.

And now upon that honoured grave,
    O'er which long years have spent,
Fair-spreading oaken branches wave ;
    True worth's best monument.

And often when the days are fair,
    Far from the city's smoke,
His children's children prattle there,
    Beneath the Soldier's Oak.

LOVE'S YOUNG DREAM.

It came again last night, love,
    That dream of home and you,
And visions of delight, love,
    Across my fancy flew ;
I dreamt I held your hand, love,
    The love-light filled your eyes ;
And wondrous schemes I plann'd, love,
    'Mid kisses, jests, and sighs.

I spoke of days to come, love,
  Of days of untold bliss,
I plann'd a little home, love,
  Where naught should move amiss.
I pressed you in my arms, love,
  And stroked your nut-brown hair,
And gazing on your charms, love,
  I thought you wondrous fair.

You pressed your cheek to mine, love,
  I vow'd I'd constant be,
And in your eyes the sign, love,
  Spoke deathless faith in me ;
I softly kissed your lips, love,
  And felt your honey'd breath,
I clasped your finger tips, love,
  And vow'd to love till death.

They come to me so oft, love,
  These dreams of home and you,
They bear my soul aloft, love,
  In yearnings sweet and new.
Keep watching every day, love,
  Till time has further flown ;
When fortune says I may, love,
  You shall be all my own.

WHEN LOVE WAS YOUNG.

I sat beside the water,
Where the sunbeams gaily danced,
In a lovely grot where soothing odours dwell ;
I watched the flecks of sunlight
As between the boughs they glanced,
Till a gush of music wandered down the dell.

I closed my eyes and listened,
And my spirit seemed to fly
From its thraldom through a mist of dreamy thoughts,
As list'ning to the music,
That on every low-breath'd sigh
Came toward me, from a thousand feather'd throats.

I lay in speechless rapture,
For they sang so wondrous sweet,
That I fancied I could give their music words ;
Till on the bending brackens
Fell the sound of lightsome feet,
And a voice that far outrivall'd all the birds.

The songsters hushed their voices,
And they listen'd quite intent,
So I rose to meet her as her tread fell near ;
She looked so very winsome
As among the trees we went,
And I breath'd the sweet old story in her ear.

LIFE'S BELLS.

Toll on ! morning bell !
Thy song in summons sweet
Calls crowds of pious feet
To matins, where they meet
   Some consolation—
       Morning Bell !

Toll on ! merry bells !
Ye tell to youthful hearts
Joy, that new life imparts
Where love to being starts,
   So sweetly sounding—
       Marriage Bells !

Toll on ! vesper bells !
Upon the evening air,
Speaking of rest from care,
Beyond the world's rude glare,
 From the grey steeple—
   Evening Bell !

Toll on ! solemn bell !
Ah ! some poor soul has gone ;
Another's work is done ;
Death calls us one by one :
 Toll thy dread message—
   Funeral Bell !

THE FLOWER OF PRIMROSE GILL.

Where the breezes waft their odours
 Over Forcett's woods and dales,
And the bracken fronds so graceful,
 Wave in flow'ret-spangled vales ;
Where the choristers of Nature
 With sweet songs the silence kill,
In the wealth of maiden sweetness
 Blooms the flower of Primrose Gill.

Nature gilds her face with smiling
   Till the streaks of mellow light,
Pressing close upon the shadow
   Puts the sullen gloom to flight.
Yet above the sunlight's glowing
   That bedecks the tree-capped hill,
In the light of heaven growing,
   Blooms the flower of Primrose Gill.

Ah ! this flower is more than earthly,
   She is human—nay, divine !
And a thousand gems less lovely
   Round about the blossom shine.
Perfumes, on the southern breezes
   Floating, Forcett's valley fill,
Yet no wood-breath scented, pleases
   Like this flower of Primrose Gill.

In some far-off grot they reared her,
   Through her young life's tender bud,
And, to Primrose Gill transplanted,
   Now she blooms to womanhood.
Far and near her fragrance floating,
   Breathes of greater sweetness still ;
And they simply call her Libby,
   This fair flower of Primrose Gill.

ORPHANS.

A sweet little maiden of five years old,
  Sat under the arbour's cooling shade,
Her hair was like tresses of waving gold,
  Through which the scented breezes played ;
On her lap she had flowers of beauty rare,
But her's was a beauty more bright, more fair.

She had roses, and asters, and pansies bright,
  And wove them in garlands about her head ;
And they cast round her features a rosy light,
  But her bright cheeks out-coloured the roses red,
And her eyes were reflections of dazzling light,
Unmatched by the stars in the dusky night.

In her breast was a feeble, full-blown rose,
  On each side of its stem was a half-oped bud ;
The old one was nigh to its evening's close,
  While the others were just in their babyhood ;
The maiden looked down with a shade in her eyes,
And a face that was clouded but wondrous wise.

'Tis written that out of the mouths of the young,
　Crey sages at times may good teachings learn,
And many a lesson from youthful tongue
　Has given philosophy's wisdom a turn ;
And now in this lovely maiden's look
Was outlined a picture from nature's book.

A breeze came and scattered the full-blown flower,
　And the petals fell at her slippered feet ;
She looked at the two remaining buds,
　And said with a smile that was, oh, so sweet !
" Two little rosebuds have opened their eyes
To kiss their mother before she dies."

WHERE ANGELS DWELL.

In a lonely, humble dwelling,
　On a little trundle bed,
Lay a mother's sunny darling,
　With blue eyes and curl-clad head ;
But alas ! that face, once sunny,
　Now was very pale and wan,
And within that form, once lively,
　Sluggish now the life-blood ran ;

While the mother and the sister
　　Wept o'er him they loved so well,
Full of hope, the dear boy murmur'd
　　Of the land where angels dwell.

" Mother ! mother, bend and kiss me,
　　Take my hand and hold it there,
When I'm gone I know you'll miss me,
　　Let me feel you stroke my hair.
Oh ! I want you near me, mother,
　　Near me now to hold my hand ;
'Twill be sweet to know you held me
　　Till I reached the unseen land.
Oh ! repeat that sweet old story,
　　That I've often heard you tell,—
Of the far-off realms of glory
　　Far away where angels dwell.

" Sometimes when I've sat and listened
　　To the stories that you told,
Underneath your eyelids glistened
　　Tears that you could scarcely hold ;
And I've heard you tell how father
　　Peacefully and calmly died,
Then I've seen your hot tears falling,
　　Though to hold them back you tried ;

Ah ! the mem'ry makes me happy,
　Happier than my tongue can tell ;
Oh ! I'll meet dear father yonder,
　Far away where angels dwell.

" There, dear mother, cease your crying,
　Do not weep, I'm going home ;
Though to you it seems so trying,—
　When they've laid me in the tomb,—
Do not weep, but keep on watching,
　List'ning through the clang of strife,
At the faintest echo catching,
　Of the summons out of life ;
I shall watch and wait, dear mother,
　While the rolling days shall swell,
Till again I meet you, mother,
　Far away where angels dwell.

" Sister, open wide the window,
　Let me breathe the scented air,
Let me see the roses tender,
　In my garden fresh and fair ;
I can see the wallflowers, mother,
　That I planted in the nook,
Oh ! I'll have to leave my garden,
　Let me take a last long look.

Tell me, mother, are there bowers
    In the realms of which you tell?
Do you think there will be flowers
    In the land where angels dwell?

" Listen ! I can hear a throstle,
    Singing near the arbour door,
Oh ! I wonder if they whistle
    In the groves on yon bright shore.
Oh ! if there are birds and blossoms
    In that land so bright and fair,
Heaven will be within the bosoms
    Of the blest who wander there.
Good-bye, wallflowers, birds, and roses !
    Oh ! I love you all so well,
But I'll be, 'ere evening closes,
    Far away where angels dwell.

" Kiss me once again, dear mother ;
    Sister kiss me, do not cry ;
Cling through life to one another,
    I will meet you by and by.
Tell my comrades I have left them,
    Never more to meet them here,
Though of me death has bereft them,
    Yet I hold their memory dear.

Give my toys to cousin Willie
    And his little sister Nell ;
Tell them I would like to meet them
    In the land where angels dwell."

Then they laid him backward gently,
    Knowing that the end was near,
And the mother and the sister
    Sobbed forth many a scalding tear ;
In that lonely, humble chamber,
    That o'erlooked the garden plot,
Someone's sun was quickly setting,
    Though the cold world knew it not ;
"Mother dear !" the sweet boy murmur'd,
    Then in death's cold sleep he fell.
Who shall say his spirit roams not,
    Somewhere where the angels dwell ?

AGAINST THE CURRENT.

I am resting on my oars !
For I've had a stubborn struggle
Hard against the tide of youth,
I have had no little trouble,
But a hard, hard time in truth ;

And I tried to bear it bravely,
Though I struggled, fought, and failed,
And I tried to take no notice
When soft smiling pleasures hailed ;
Once I near went down the rapids,
Where that dark destruction roars,
But I battled till I conquer'd—
Now I'm resting on my oars.

I am resting on my oars !
Soon I'll strike with greater vigour—
Bend and pull with greater will ;
Soon I'll have to breast the breakers
That will sorely test my skill ;
But I'll grip again and wrestle,
And I'll cut the waves' white crest,
Then when I have gained the harbour,
Oh ! how sweet will be my rest ;
If I cannot brave the billows,
If too high the tempest roars,
Father ! hasten to my succour,
God of goodness grip the oars !

FAIRY DELL.

There's a path along the valley,
  Winding through the bushy thorns,
Where the brooklet sweetly gurgles
  Near the feather-looking ferns.
Where the sunshine through the branches,
  Gleams in checks of light and shade,
And the perfumes softly wander,
  Scenting all the lovely glade.

Musing, down the path I saunter,
  And I hear the vesper bells,
Singing from the old grey steeple,
  And the music sinks and swells ;
Dying down the wooded valley,
  Comes the throstle's silver call,
And it mingles with the music
  Of the tingling water-fall.

When the south wind sweetly rustles
  Through the foliage up the steep,
And the timid goldfinch whistles
  In the brushwood dark and deep.

There I watch the sunlight flicker,
    Up the silver wimpling stream,
And my cares are deeply buried
    In a beautiful day-dream.

There I sometimes meet a maiden,
    Singing like a bird in spring,
With the voice that holds me spell-bound,
    As it makes the echoes ring ;
And this maiden's such a fairy,
    Loving this sweet spot so well,
That I could not help but name it,
    So I call it Fairy Dell.

SAINT ANDREW'S BELLS.*

"Twas the day of rest and quiet,
    That calm day so bright and fair,
When the heart with inborn rapture swells ;
    And methought a spirit wandered
    On the solemn Sabbath air,
As I listened to Saint Andrew's bells.

* St Andrew's, South Church, near Bishop Auckland.

What a flood of music floated
From the tower dim and grey !
How it wandered down the leafy dells !
What a languor o'er me settled,
That calm, sorrow-soothing day,
As I listened to Saint Andrew's bells !

Sweetly sighing o'er the pasture ;
Softly singing through the wood ;
Where the woodbine, clinging, sweetly smells :
And my heart in speechless rapture
Swelled my bosom as I stood,
Calmly list'ning to Saint Andrew's bells.

Downy sparrows ceased their chatter,
And the village all was hushed
In that quiet which of sweet rest tells ;
And I fancied all were list'ning
To the music as it gushed
From the throats of sweet Saint Andrew's bells.

Busy Auckland, in the distance,
Was for once quite mute and calm,
And a zephyr came across the woods and fells ;
And methought a spirit lingered
Breathing out a heavenly balm,
As I listened to Saint Andrew's bells.

BEAUTIFUL MAY.

There's music and perfume afloat in the air :
    There's sunshine and flowers on the land ;
There's stillness and sweetness beyond compare,
    For nature has opened her hand ;
There's shadow and light in the depths of the woods,
    And the birds are sweet-throated and gay,
And all beauteous nature re-echoes the words—
        " Beautiful, beautiful May !"

There's budding and blooming in vales and on hills,
    And softly the southern winds play ;
There's tingling and dancing of playful rills,
    That career o'er their pebble-strewn way ;
There's flower-spangled mantles of emerald green,
    Wide-spreading o'er pastures away,
And on every bough thy traces are seen,
        " Beautiful, beautiful May !"

There's fresh-bursting hawthorn on every hedge,
    And fresh-sprouting corn in the fields ;
There's tracks on the sand by the river's edge,
    And the spirit to indolence yields.

There's languor and haze in the softly-breathed air,
  And the lambs o'er the green hillocks play.
Oh ! sweet hawthorn month, thou art cheery and fair,
  " Beautiful, beautiful May !"

JOURNEYING ON.

Your wrinkles are deepening, my darling,
  The years have frost-tinted your hair,
And under those dear eyes, my darling,
  Are limned the rude footprints of care.
Long, long have we battled together,
  And breasted the buffets and frowns ;
Through stormy and troublesome weather
  We've battled the ups and the downs.

We met in the spring-tide, my darling,
  Our lives were just bursting in leaf ;
We bloomed through the summer, my darling,
  And autumn beset us with grief.
Our life-stem was ruthlessly shaken,
  And she whom we cherished so dear,
Our first-fruit, was blighted and taken :
  We mourned through the winter so drear.

Look out of the window, my dearest,
   Where oft we've stood gazing before,
That mound to the porch lying nearest—
   As though 'twould be in at the door—
There slumbers the sun of our summer,
   The flower that we nourished and watched,
Our bright, blue-eyed fireside angel,
   That nought in our minds ever matched.

Oh ! don't you remember the robin
   That hopped o'er the crisp frozen snow,
And sang his sweet songs to our lost one,
   That Christmas day, long, long ago ?
And don't you remember the blackbird,
   When spring had returned once again ?
He sang in the tall leafy poplar,
   A cheery and heart-stirring strain.

And years since that time have fled o'er us,
   The summers have budded and gone,
And friends have departed before us,
   The old forms have fled one by one.
You weep, wife ! well, well, it is better,
   These tears will relieve your fond heart ;
Our time will come sooner or later—
   Contented and calmly we'll part.

If I should go first, oh ! my darling !
   And meet our dear daughter up there,
I'll tell her her mother is coming,
   I'll bid all the old friends prepare.
And down from our Heaven we'll watch you,
   And when you are ready to come
Heaven's arches shall echo the welcome—
   " Come home, faithful spirit, come home !"

— · —

A SPRING SONG.

Look at the blended gold and roses
   Up in the sunlit morning sky ;
See how the early dawn discloses
   Tints that the painter's arts defy.
Over the hill top, Phœbus gleaming
   Winks in the face of dewy morn,
And the roseate ribbons streaming,
   Are as the heralds of Spring new-born.

Come to the meadows where the daisies
    Open their eyes to behold the sun,
Where a thousand floral beauties
    Plainly tell us the Spring's begun.
Come to the brook and watch its waters
    Ripple and dance with a music sweet,
And it will tell us the Spring is throwing
    Garlands of beauty before our feet.

Come to the woods, and you'll hear the thrushes
    Rustle and sing through the branches bare,
Down in the mazy entangled bushes,
    Singing of Spring's rich mantle there.
Balmy and sweet is the fragrant breathing
    Of the sweet goddess of hazy morn ;
And the fair fields are busily wreathing
    Garlands to crown the Spring new-born.

ONLY A YEAR AND A DAY.

'Tis only a year and a day, sweet maiden,
    Since you gave your heart to me,
Down where the arbour with flowers was laden,
    As we sat 'neath the maple tree.
Well I remember the silver evening—
    'Twas one of these balmy eves of June—
And up in the grey-blue over the orchard
    Was plainly apparent the feeble moon ;
      As we sat in the maple's shade,
      Watching the daylight fade,
Two hearts as one united, a year and a day gone by.

Only a year and a day, my darling !
    Don't you remember the red rose-bud
That I plucked in the stillness and placed in your bosom,
    How that token was understood ?
You cannot have ceased to remember those kisses
    I drank from your lips as the night sped on !
And still as sweet are those fond caresses
    As ever they were in the days that are gone,
      When we sat in the arbour's shade,
      Watching the daylight fade,
Two hearts so fondly plighted, a year and a day gone by.

Only a year and a day, my affianced,
    Oh, the sweet memory it brings!
Hallowed remembrance of hours long flitted,
        How they vibrate on my heart-strings!
And, oh! the eye language that set my heart panting,
    As I pressed to my bosom your dainty glove!
I found a something I'd long been wanting;
    That something, my darling, was your fond love.
        Which you gave in the maple's shade,
        While we watched the daylight fade,
That lovely summer evening, a year and a day gone by.

DAWN.

Far to eastward breaks the dawning,
    O'er the dim horizon line,
And the parting shadows, yawning,
    Show a fair day's golden sign;
Back in fright, the dim clouds, breaking,
    Give their place to Phœbus' light;
And the rose-hued morning, streaking,
    Bursts o'er earth in beauty bright.

Now it gilds the distant mountains,
   Nearer, nearer, o'er the vale;
Now it skimmers on the fountains,
   Tinting forest, hill, and dale;
Now it streaks the brook with beauty,
   Checkered through the willows tall,
Till it seems like molten silver,
   Hurrying o'er the narrow fall.

Now adown the valley rushing,
   Where erewhile dwelt darkness black,
Where the pimpernell is blushing,
   Hard upon the shadow's track;
Drinking up the dews of morning,
   Golden sunlight treads apace,
And at last the fair-faced dawning
   Spreads the whole of Nature's face.

SILVER OR GOLD.*

Seventeen summers have softly scattered
   Sweet summer blossoms on thy fair head ;
Now thy young life's in its fragrant morning,
   Long may it be ere thy beauty has fled !
What though the years in prospective bring changes,
   What though the locks which are gold shall turn grey
Roaming together 'mong pilgrims and strangers,
   Shall we in future love less than to day ?
      Nay ! I will love thee when thou art old ;
      Yes ! I will love thee
   When there is silver in place of the gold.

Golden-hued now are thy shimmering tresses,
   Framing in sweetness thy peachy cheeks,
Yet thou wilt e'er find the same my caresses,
   E'en when that hair shows the silvery streaks.

---

   * A poem by L. S. Upham was published in the *Weekly
Budget*, May 8th, 1875, which gave rise to this.   In sending
my verses to the *Newcastle Weekly Chronicle*, I acknow-
ledged the fact, but they omitted the acknowledgment.
                    J. R. W.

Now thou art crowned with the sweet orange blossoms,
   And on thy hand is the bridal ring,
Think not, my own, that into this bosom
   Changes of years shall dull coldness bring,
     For I will love thee when thou art old ;
       Yes ! I will love thee
    When there is silver in place of the gold.

Gladly I give thee the loving assurance ;
   What canst thou ask I would give thee beside ?
Fondly I take thee, for richer for poorer,
   And on life's ocean together we'll glide.
When life's December shall find those locks hoary,
   E'en when our frames to the winter-blasts bow ;
Blooming the same as in summer's day glory,
   Loved shalt thou be the same then as now :
     Yes ! I will love thee when thou art old ;
      Still will I love thee
    When there is silver in place of the gold.

BEHOLD THY WORK!

Seducer, mark the wreck which thou has made,
 And let the sight bring down that haughty look.
Oh ! why does conscience not thyself upbraid
 At sight of that which thou, blind fool, mistook,
And led thy mind to think 'twere but a toy
 To lift, to look on, and to put aside ;
A sudden, pleasant, flitting, earthly joy.
 Far better, than have met thee, had she died !

Far better had she never known the curse
 Of such a love as thine, whose ingrate power
Has made her trusting heart a something worse
 Than ever entered into shame's dark bower.
Dead to the world, she dares not raise her head
 To mortal gaze, but hides her blushing face
As though she were to silent sorrow wed,
 Beneath the burden of a fell disgrace !

Look ! fell destroyer, look ! and mark that eye
  Whose blighted beauty lacks that sudden fire
With which it glowed till doomed to wane and die
  By thy most foul and uncontrolled desire !
Fiend in human form ! whose subtle tongue
  Lured on and led her to this burning shame ;
Whose wily, cunning arts and scheming wrong
  Robbed her of that she held so dear, her name !

Base coward ! of the deepest, blackest stain !
  Canst thou not find in all thy dastard heart
One spark of pity for the rankling pain
  Of which what thou dost see is but a part ?
Think, when she found thee traitor to thy trust,
  Herself betrayed, and thou, the baser man,
A perjured paltry thing, whose greedy lust
  Leads him to seize a victim when he can !

Oh ! what could her stained bosom hope for then ?
  When friends and foes alike spoke of her shame,
And made her feel distrustful hate of men,
  When, scoundrel ! thou alone art but to blame.
Oh, folly's slave ! whose soul-revolting deed
  Hast proved thee what thou art, creation's scum !
Is't in thy mind, however great thy need,
  To hope for favour in the world to come ?

Why turn away and shun that blighted flower,
   Once pure and spotless in her Maker's eyes,
Whom thou hast made before those eyes to cower,
   And found, alas, a ready sacrifice ?
Man ! should the title not the truth belie,   .
   Wilt thou not save her whom the fates deride,
Now cast upon the world, perchance to die
   A wretched and heart-broken suicide ?

ANNIE OF UPSALL GROVE.

Once when I sojourned 'mid scenes well remembered,
   In summer's soft beauty, 'neath Hambleton's shade,
I daily drank in each fair flower's inspiration
   In groves where the linnets at hide and seek played.
Yet sweeter than flow'rets and fairer than linnets,
   As bright as the sunbeams that gilded the brook,
There came in my pathway a golden-haired maiden
   Whose soul seemed outspoken in every look ;
And she seemed just the creature the heart chords to move.
      And my heart sometimes tries
      To remember the eyes
        Of Annie of Upsall Grove.

True, she was youthful ; too young to learn loving ;
    So chaste and so lovely, so childishly gay ;
Yet sweetest of girlhood on this wide earth moving,
    Though young, she will grow to a woman one day.
Ah ! may be, by this time her beauty has glided
    From girlhood's sweet bud to a woman's rich bloom,
For in her fair face all the light was provided,
    To break forth in sunshine and brighten the gloom.
Still I think of the time when 'gainst loving I strove.
        And my heart sometimes tries
        To recall the bright eyes
        Of Annie of Upsall Grove.

STAGE STRUCK.*

He chalked out a path for his after-days,
And flattered himself that the world's strange ways
    Were unerringly known to him ;
And wild were the fancies that filled his breast
Of money and mirth, and among the rest
    A glory that nought could dim.

*Written on the *debut* of a young man of Houghton-le-Spring.

He pictured himself on a great bare stage ;
Imagined himself in a tragic rage ;
    A flourish of steel and a fall ;
A flood of blue light as if from the clouds ;
The roaring applause of admiring crowds,
    That echoed from wall to wall.

And oft, in the depth of his humble den,
He thought to himself how the newspaper men
    Would " puff" him from week to week.
These "puffs" he would read to himself, word for word,
And again he would swing an imaginary sword,
    And shout till he scarce could speak.

He went and engaged : the die was cast,
And the curtain arose on his face at last ;
    He trembled and hung his head ;
In the heat of the moment he lost his cue,
And a voice, that rung his senses through,
    Invited him home to bed.

He slunk from the stage in an awful plight,
And quickly as possible slunk out of sight,
    And speedily altered his plan.
That one stage-flood had quenched his fire,
And so he went back to his native mire
    A sadder and wiser man.

A WAIF.

Cold! cold! cold!
So cold, and so weak, and so worn;
In the midnight hush when the shops are shut,
 And the lamps, too, ill illume the street,
Crouching behind a water-butt
 With bare, and blue, and bleeding feet,
In a dark and lonely city court
A woman sits in the damp and the dirt,
 So cold, and so weak, and so worn.

Weak! weak! weak!
So wretched, so weak, and so worn;
Battered and bruised by the world's rude strife;
 Goaded to shame by the cold world's sneers;
Stabbed by the many reverses of life,
 Faint and forsaken she sits in her tears;
Down in the mire of black misery hurled,
Sneered at and spurned by a haughty world,
 So wretched, so weak, and so worn.

Damp! damp! damp!
So dirty, so damp, and so numb;
Unheeded, uncared for, she moans her lot,
 Forsaken and friendless, and dying there.

In the broad daylight we beheld her not ;
  We saw not the matted and grey-grown hair,
We heard not her plea in the crowded street;
  We saw not the swollen and blue-cold feet
    So dirty, so damp, and so numb !

    Faint ! faint ! faint '
  So famished, so faint, and so wan ;
With eyes sad and sunken, and blurred and red,
  She shudders and starts to her blistered feet,
And hanging the weary dejected head
  She paces the dreary, deserted street
All through the long night till the early morn,
Then another long day with the world's cold scorn,
  So famished, so faint, and so wan !

    Dead ! dead ! dead !
  So solemn, so silent, and still ;
With no one to weep near the cold, calm head ;
  At length she sinks under the 'whelming wave,
They take her away to the home of the dead,
  And she finds a sweet rest in a pauper's grave.
A woman,—and oh ! we heard not her cry,
But we left her alone, sad and silent to die ;
  So solemn, so silent, so still !

A FIRESIDE ANGEL.

(An Imagination.)

It might have been real, but it was more like a dream to me, when I saw that old man and his old dame, they were not wrinkled, but their hair was silvered. Between them sat a fairy-looking maid, with sunny hair and heaven-blue eyes. There seemed to be a life-tie connecting the three; the old man seemed to regard the maid as heaven-sent. He might have been in his dotage, but it was a strange happy state; and I could'nt help regarding the maiden in the same light as did this grey-haired couple. Sometimes I fancy there must have been reality in it, and yet I am compelled to admit that it is imagination. "Whence did she come?" I asked; and the old man drew the golden head on his breast, and, smiling, replied to my query :—

" She came from the land of the setting sun,
　Borne to us in a flood of gold,
And long ere she could talk or run,
　Her future had the beldames told ;

From heaven she winged down through the air,
And came to soothe our worldly care;
From whence you see yon lovely streaks of blue,
She caught her eye-tint as she floated through.

"She came from the land of the One in Three,
    To gladden hearts, illume the hearth,
And fill our souls with boundless glee,
    And make the fireside ring with mirth;
Down from the wide and shining dome
She came to light our earthly home;
From where you see yon gilt-floods spreading fair
She caught the colour of her sunny hair.

"She came from the land of the lovely blue,
    And brought with her our second life;
She came the fleecy cloudlets through,
    Between us and a world of strife.
Down from the mighty shining vast
To us her gentle soul was cast;
From where the sky yon soft vermilion tips
She caught the colour of those florid lips.

"She came from the home of the angels bright,
    Borne to us on fair angel wings;
She came and made our darkness light,
    And now she gaily trips and sings.

A world of sunbeams lights her face,
Her every look's a look of grace,
From where you see yon spreading pinky streaks
She stole the colour of her waxen cheeks.

"She came from the land of the promised bliss,
    And drove the gloom from out our hearts;
Her nature did the soft clouds kiss,
    Thus giving her those winsome arts.
Her childish prattle's constant flow
Reminds us of the long ago;
From where the angels chant their hallowed strain
She came, and thither will return again."

The old man paused; the old dame smiled. Truly,
I thought, we have angels on the hearth, and I
recalled to mind a home-angel I had seen, caring
tenderly for a reeling, bleared drunkard once; I
thought of the fathers and the brothers who daily,
hourly, martyr these "angels of the hearth."
Looking at this fairy creature now, I asked,
"*When did* she come?" and the old dame replied:—

"She came when the daisies decked the plain
    And sunny was the spring-tide air,
When blackbirds sang their mellow strain
    And early flowers were bright and fair.

When brightly shone the smiling east,
And Nature held her spring-tide feast,
When soft spring brightness filled the verdant earth,
She drove the dulness from our lonely hearth

"She came when the cowslip reared its head
    To meet the monarch of the morn,
When fields were by the bright dew fed,
    And budding was the sweet hawthorn;
When o'er the fields was heard to float
The cuckoo's life-enlivening note,
When gorgeous Phœbus did the earth illume
Her cooing voice dispelled the sullen gloom.

"She came when the linnet gaily sang,
    And sparrows chirruped o'er the lea,
When every wood with music rang,
    And brooklets bubbled merrily,
When on the hedges might be seen
The tender shoots of lively green,
When zephyrs brought the breath of Twizell Grove,
She burst upon us, claiming all our love."

MOWBRAY'S BONNIE VALE.

'Mong Upsall's bonnie vales and woods,
　　In balmy hush of silver Spring,
I ofttimes watch the sunny floods
　　That shimmer where the linnet sings ;
Down by some wimpling, purling brook,
　　That tinkles o'er a pebbled bed,
And whirls through many a hidden nook ;
　　Here by my yearning fancy led,
I wander 'mong the stately groves of ash and elm
　　trees tall,
Where eddying wavelets trickle down a mossy
　　waterfall.

Up where the heather's furzy growth
　　Gives shelter to the moorland fowl,
· That skims black Hambleton's wild crown,
　　High towering by sweet Kirby Knowle ;

Or where dame Nature's handiwork
    Smiles Yorkshire's sweetest scenes upon,
Down by picturesque Feliskirk,
    Or up the hill to Mount St. John ;
Sweet scenes that often lure the heart forth from its
    prison-breast,
Of all the views of beauty, Mowbray's bonnie Vale's
    the best.

To barter smiles for cheerless gloom,
    Thine is the power, life-giving grot ;
Far distant be the sordid doom
    That changing, would enhance thee not ;
And when again I quit thy bowers,
    Be mine the tongue to speak thy praise ;
The birds, the trees, the hills, the flowers,
    Remembered be for length of days ;
Where'er I roam, in coming time, whatever be my
    lot,
Thy scenes, sweet Vale of Mowbray, shall never be
    forgot !

SONNET TO RICHARD ABBOT.

Author of War, and other Poems.

To thee, fair Forcett's bard, all I can give
Is given here, a kindred soul's regard ;
Returned affection is the best reward
That heart to heart can offer ; may'st thou live
To prove the firmness of the hand I give
In fondest friendship.   Since I spent with thee
Hours, far too short-lived, of enjoyment free,
No brighter hours that my heart can conceive
Could in their brightness e'er out-glimmer these
I spent with thee beneath the Autumn trees.
Long as this life shall last, and memory stand
In my poor brain, thou shalt remembered be :
And when the end shall come, in yon fair land
Above the vastness, may I meet with thee.

E

NATURE SURPASSED.

I culled a primrose in the evening's hush.
    Lost in the sweetness of the song-dipped wood ;
The setting sun diffused a rosy blush,
    And bathed the woodland in a golden flood.
I placed the primrose in her midnight hair,
    'Twas like a star-gleam in the distant sky,
Missioned it seemed to watch her face so fair,
    But lost its lustre matched with her bright eye.

PRAY FOR THE POOR.

Hark ! my love, how the wind is howling !
    Think of the mariners out to night,
Toiling upon the lashing waters,
    While we sit by the warm fire-light.
Think of the houseless, footsore wand'rers,
    Wrestling along the road of life.
Let us thank God for home, my darling,
    Let us pray for the poor, my wife.

Think, my love, of the friendless children
  Slowly dying of want and cold ;
Draw your babe close up to your bosom,
  Treasure her there as wealth untold.
Think of the many departing daily,
  Unwept out of the world of strife.
Let us thank God for enough, my darling,
  Let us pray for the poor, my wife.

WHEN THE LILAC WAS IN BLOOM.

Long ago she met me there,
And I watched her face so fair,
  When the lilac was in bloom ;
And she blushed a rosebud hue,
As she vow'd she would be true.
  No fair flow'ret's sweet perfume
With her sweet breath could compare,
As I stroked her nut-brown hair,
  When the lilac was in bloom.

Leaning on the terrace wall,
Listening to the blackbird's call,
  When the lilac was in bloom.

In the grove beneath our feet
Wood flowers lent their fragrance sweet :
　　Sinking sunlight did illume
Sombre yews and poplars tall,
By the fountain's crystal fall,
　　When the lilac was in bloom.

And when last I saw her there
Silver mingled with her hair,
　　When the lilac was in bloom ;
And her joyous laugh was hushed,
Yet she softly, sweetly blushed ;
　　Still those giant poplars loom
Skyward in the evening air,
Still her face, though grave, is fair,
　　And the lilac is in bloom.

THOSE EYES.

There's love in those speaking eyes ;
Eyes like the fair forget-me-not
That hides its head in yon sylvan grot,
Companion of violets, whose sweet perfume
Co-mingles with that of the lilac bloom !
　　　　Liquid Eyes !

There's hope in those dreamy eyes ;
A shadow of hope, whose pellucid gleam
Adds tint to the gold of thy "love's young dream";
Eyes that by sorrow were never yet dimmed ;
Eyes that no painter as yet truly limned ;
   Beauteous Eyes !

There's *something* in those soft eyes ;
A *something*, a *nothing*,—I know not what,—
A river of sweetness ; Nay ! more than that ;
A tenderness hid under silken lids,
A look that invites me and yet forbids ;
   Wondrous Eyes !

There's life in those lovely eyes ;
Life for the heart that's so truly thine,
Moulded and worked to thine own design ;
Fashioned to love thee while life shall burn ;
Struggling thy deep hidden yearnings to learn,
   From those Eyes !

THE FIRST SNOW FLAKES.

Cold blows across the moor the shrieking blast,
　　Whirling in demon glee the leaves so dead ;
Autumn's soft richness quickly hurries past ;
　　All the rich hue from Nature's face is fled ;
The keenly cutting wind to whispers deep
　　Sinks his chill breath and blights the last frail bough ;
And earthward on the veering currents sweep,
　　In feathered throng, the first white flakes of snow.

Softly they fall out of the distance dim,
　　As seeming myriads of swerving specks,
Now nearer hurrying, large and larger grow,
　　As on the earth they fall in fleecy flecks,
Whit'ning the frozen roadway as they fall,
　　Thickening and drifting into corners deep,
Gathering in down-like wreaths upon the wall,
　　Down wind-swept alleys on the blast they sweep.

On the church tower's grey head a soft white cap
  Rests, thickening as the snow flakes still descend.
There only to remain in state, mayhap,
  Till less cold breezes wand'ring thither wend.
With the soft breathing of a warmer hour,
  From the low cottage in its ivy drest,
From the bare hedgerow and the lofty tower,
  Melt the first snowflakes of the winter's vest.

DRAMATIS PERSONÆ.

THE CURTAIN UP.

Face to the audience,
  Pacing the stage,
Pictures of gentleness,
  Models of rage ;
Martyrs to honour
  Bleeding for truth ;
Middle-aged women
  Ardent in youth ;

Natural slovens
   Looking so neat;
Sour-visaged women
   "Doing" the sweet;
Men, poor and needy,
   Rolling in wealth;
Men who are robust
   Out of their health;
Young man, consumptive,
   Strong as a horse;
Heir to a fortune,
   Naught in his purse;
Man, aged thirty,
   Wrinkled and grey;
Woman of fifty
   Youthful and gay;
Man who hates music
   Yearning to sing;
Journeyman tailor
   Raised to be king;
Masculine woman
   Meek as a dove;
Man who dislikes her
   Dying for love;
Man who is little
   Looking so big;

Bald-headed gentleman
  Sporting a wig ;
Horrible murder,
  Trial in town,
Death on the scaffold :
  Curtain goes down.

THE CURTAIN DOWN.

Back of the canvas,
  In the green room ;
Women, so pleasant,
  Pictures of gloom ;
Truth's bleeding martyrs,
  Lies all they say ;
Lovely young women
  Fast turning grey ;
Spruce-looking ladies
  Dowdy and loose ;
Sweet-looking creatures
  Sour as the deuce ;
Man with the fortune
  Hasn't a " mag,"
Doffs off his broadcloth
  On with his rag ;

Healthy young farmer
　Rubs off his paint,
Shows a grim visage
　Pallid and faint ;
Man with the whiskers—
　Curly black hair—
Proves to be ginger,
　Face nearly bare ;
Woman in satin
　Pulls off her dress,
Pulls on her cotton,
　Looks in distress ;
Man with the helmet,
　In battle used,
Dons his " three shillings'-worth,"
　Sadly abused ;
Man who gave dinners,
　Balls, and soirees,
Goes to his supper—
　Porter and cheese ;
Man who was single
　Boasts of a wife ;
Man who was murder'd
　Comes back to life.

CHANGED.

Gone are the golden hours ;
  Fallen the fresh green leaves ;
Gone are my heart's first flowers,
  And Time's reaper a garland weaves ;
A garland of fading blossoms
  Inwoven with wilted grass ;
A garland of yellowing laurels
  That grow bare as the winds go past.

Gone are the perfumed zephyrs ;
  Gone are the pearls of dew ;
Hushed are those still small voices
  That went thrilling my bosom through ;
Dead are the balmy bygones ;
  Hushed is each birdling's song ;
Quiet and mute is the music ;
  And the shadows around me throng.

Dead are the fairy faces ;
   Mute are the sounds of mirth ;
Gone are the youthful graces,
   And the pleasures have lost their worth ;
But there remains a darling,
   One whom I took for life,
Life of my soul, I'll struggle
   For her through the mists and strife.

LIZZETTE.

I am lonely now without thee,
   This world has no charms for me ;
Night and day I think about thee,
   In my dreams thy form I see ;
" Father ! where've they put poor mamma ?"
   Asks our lisping, blue-eyed pet ;
And I never fail to tell him,
   Thou art gone to heaven, Lizzette !

Oh! what anguish fills my bosom;
  Oh! what memories I recall,
When I see our dear child gazing
  At thy portrait on the wall;
Just last night he sat beside me,
  And I never can forget,
Every feature seemed to tell me,
  Oh! he's like my dead Lizzette.

When upon his knees at bedtime,
  Uttering his simple prayer,
Every syllable he uttered
  Made me think that thou wert there ;
Oh! he seemed so very earnest,
  And his eyes with tears were wet,
When he murmur'd, "God bless mamma!"
  Oh, I burst in tears, Lizzette!

Oh! I'm lonely now without thee,
  And the hours drag slowly now;
Every thing I see about me,
  Brings the grief-cloud o'er my brow;
Yet I am not quite despairing,
  Not quite hope-forsaken yet;
Something tells me we shall meet thee
  In the land unseen, Lizzette.

BONNIE KIRBY KNOWLE.

Fast by Upsall's age-worn walls,
  Bathed in moonlight's gilding glow,
Where her mate the wood-bird calls,
  Where tall firs sway to and fro,
      Sleeps bonnie Kirby Knowle ;
Sheltered by the bare, brown moors
That skyward loom in eastern glow,
      Bonnie Kirby Knowle !

Flooded in the noontide hush
  Of a silver-gilding sun,
Where the heather's rosy blush
  Tints the hours that slowly run,
      I've seen thee, Kirby Knowle !
When the sweet, spring-laden breeze
To waft its fragrance had begun,
      Bonnie Kirby Knowle !

Swallow'd in a mellow calm,
   Matchless beauty veils thy face ;
Thine the scenes made sorrows balm.
   At the grim moor's fir-fringed base,
      Sleep on sweet Kirby Knowle !
'Mid thy woods of dingy hue,
The light and shade each other chase.
      Bonnie Kirby Knowle !

Peaceful may thy future be,
   Rich with beauty, ever bright,
From despoiling art held free,
   Ever lovely to the sight,
      Remain, sweet Kirby Knowle !
Seeming still more bright and fair,
While passing ages wing their flight,
      Bonnie Kirby Knowle !

"BREAD'S PROMISED AND WATER'S SURE."

Though under the ban of Dame Fortune's frowns.
 And ruffled by cold reverses,
We'll battle together the ups and the downs,
 That for us our destiny nurses ;
We've poverty's consolation at least,
 If we're not possessed of a cure,
"Enough," be assured, "is as good as a feast ;"
 "Bread's promised and water's sure."

Come, cheer up, my wife, and be hopeful still,
 And look to the side that is brightest,
To see us die isn't the Master's will,
 Although our load be none the lightest ;
We'll always have clothing to cover our bones.
 And what else we need is secure,
A picture of hope is here painted for us,
 "Bread's promised and water's sure."

We were driven away from the rich man's gates
   When with crumbs we'd have been contented ;
But yet there's a great day of reck'ning awaits,
   And if the sin be not repented,
Fine linen and purple will nothing avail ;
   And if we but firmly endure
We never shall want, for "the Lord will provide ; "
   " Bread's promised and water's sure."

A FAREWELL.

   I looked up the sunlit glade,
And tho' I could not speak, yet a sad farewell
Went out from my soul up that bosky dell,
And it spoke to the blossoms, the birds, and the bees,
And they answered again on the murmuring breeze,
     " Farewell ! "

   I looked up the flower-decked fields,
And I saw the white cot at the foot of the hill,
And the path down the meadow that led to the mill :
As the brook hurried on o'er its time-worn track,
I sobbed a good-bye, and it answered back,
     " Farewell ! "

F

I passed by the yellow cliff,
Where the sheet of clear water precipitate fell,
I shook off a tear and I said " Farewell!"
The water was roaring and dashing headlong,
Yet I fancy it said in its ceaseless song,
   " Farewell!"

I turned my gaze on the school,
The spot where my boyish days were spent,
And around my heart a wild thrill it sent ;
I said " Farewell!" and the heart-wrung cry
Was echoed again on a low sad sigh,—
   " Farewell!"

I turned to the grey-grown church,
And my glance wandered in at the open door,
To the things that perchance I would never see more,
And the memory smote to my heart its pain ;
I sigh'd a good-bye, and it answered again,
   " Farewell!"

I stood 'mid the silent dead,
And a tear stole down my burning cheek,
And I looked the farewell I could not speak ;
And a voice seemed to come from my comrade's tomb,
And it said, "I am waiting to welcome you home,—
   " Farewell!"

I stood on the vessel's deck,
And the hand of her I so dearly loved
With a farewell kiss from her bright lips moved ;
Oh ! I almost fancied I heard her sigh,
And my sorrowing heart welled up in the cry,
" Farewell ! "

I stood on the foreign shore,
And my eyes wandered over the wide expanse,
And the sea and the sky returned my glance ;
But over the waves came a migrate bird,
And it bore to my fancy the wondrous word—
" Farewell ! "

LOVE'S INVITATION.

See, yonder is the moon !
Stealing from her satin bedding,
Smiling, blushing, like a bride,
From the flurry of a wedding,
At her ardent husband's side.
Let us leave the streets, my darling,
Leave the city's din and strife,
And we'll wander through the meadows,
Talking of our after-life ;

I will whisper of devotion,
   You shall wrap your soul in dreams,
Love itself shall be the potion,
   And the light of yon soft beams
Shall illume your pathway, darling,   ·
   By the side of tingling streams !
Come then, darling, come to the meadows,
   Where the calm and scented breeze
Breathes its soothing spirit whispers
     Through the trees !

    Look where the silver moon
Leaves the satin clouds behind her,
   Hurrying up the spangled vast
To illume the wooded valley,
   And upon its brooklet cast
Beams that far outvie the jewels
   Of the city's favoured maid.
You shall see those beams, my darling,
   Lighting up the bosky glade ;
You will hear the cushat calling
   To his mate far up the dell ;
And a thousand night-sounds falling,
   Where poetic fancies dwell,
Will enchant your ear, my darling,
   Where the half-hushed music's swell.

Come then, dearest, come to the valley,
    Where the calm and sleepy breeze
Pipes a thousand fairy murmurs
    Through the trees !

    See how the smiling moon
Bids us leave the stir and bustle,
    Bids us fly the homes of men,
To the spot where south winds rustle
    Through the shadow-freckled glen.
Come ! and I'll renew with fervour
    Every fond affection's pledge,
And we'll hear the brook's soft murmur
    As he winds among the sedge ;
I will tell you tales of daring,
    How, for love of maidens' eyes,
Men have thrown their lives in danger,
    Scorned, when women were the prize ;
Come ! I'll tell you all the yearning
    Of a love that never dies.
Come then, dearest, roam in the moonlight,
    Where the fancy-waking breeze
Wafts the sound of Nature's music
    Through the trees !

THE CUT DIRECT.

A lordling, heart-stabbed, to a gipsy-maid stooping,
  In her listening ear did the honeyed naught breathe;
She meanwhile, her head (crowned with raven hair)
        drooping,
  Seemed eager and gladly the vows to receive.
He spoke of his castle, his lands, and his carriage,
  And tempted the bird with a baiting of gold;
He spoke of the continent, hinted at marriage,
  And attempted to kiss her, by silence made bold.

At that, like a tiny volcano, she bursted,
  And upturned her nose at his offer of pelf;
His encircling arm away from her she thrusted,
  And brought the proud libertine back to himself;
And then, like a turkey whose crest had been ruffled,
  She stood on her guard, from the gold trance awake;
The haughty one stared, lower'd his eye-glass and
        shuffled,
  And seemed to remember he'd made a mistake.

"Away, sir !" she cried, "get thee back to thy people,
  And pick up some milky-faced child of thy kind.
And think, when thy gold at her feet thou dost offer.
  A gipsy-maid spurned it and cast it behind ;
Go back to thy splendour, I spurn all thy offers,
  Go back to the prison made bright by thy gold,
Another I love, and I'll share what he suffers,
  Go from me, and blush for the tale thou hast told !"

HEAVEN-BLUE EYES.

We sat 'neath the shade of the drooping laburnum.
  When thy winsome face was with blushes aglow.
And those lips, so sweet, were a lovely vermilion,
  As we strolled down the path where the roses blow;
Oft, in the glow of the sun's matchless grandeur,
  Hours I passed in the fairy-like grot,
Feasting my eyes on thy form's regal splendour,
  The fast-flying moments I noticed not ;
And with thine did I mingle my yearnings and sighs,
      For I loved thee so truly !
      So fondly and truly !
And all for the wealth of those heaven-blue eyes.

We walked on the banks of the whispering river,
    And softly inaudible nothings we spoke ;
'Twas there that I promised to love thee for ever,
    And the voice of the wood-bird the echoes awoke.
How well I remember the soul-thrilling whispers
    That sent a wild tremor down into my heart !
And in fancy I hear the village bells pealing
    As they burst on our ears as we turned to depart;
And with thine did I mingle my hopes and my joys,
        For I loved thee so truly !
        So fondly and truly !
And all for the wealth of those heaven-blue eyes.

And dost thou remember the soft summer morning,
    What a halo of bliss o'er our nuptials was thrown ?
With the bright orange-blossoms thy fair head adorning,
    To the altar I led thee to make thee my own.
And dost thou remember those vows at the altar,
    The promise I gave from the depths of my heart
For ever and ever to love and to cherish,
    In sickness or sorrow, till death us do part?
Still with thine do I mingle my yearnings and sighs,
        For I love thee so truly !
        So fondly and truly !
And all for the wealth of those heaven-blue eyes.

EQUAL TO THE OCCASION.

A bonnie Scotch lassie cam' merrily dancin',
  Sae cheerie an' winsome, adown a green loan,
The light o' her twa bonnie een gaily glancin';
  An' blithely she sang wi' a silvery tone.
Some yards in the rear, leukin' unco dejected,
  A lazy auld donkey cam' trudgin' alang,
Wi' lugs prickit up an' recht forrard directed,
  Just as though listenin' intent tae the sang.

A fiery-haired gawky cam' cheerily whistlin'
  An' smilin' a' ower his sandy phizog;
The tow on his head like a porcupine bristlin',
  As onward he moved 'twixt a hop and a jog.
"Maw lassie," said Sandie, "ye're cheerfu' this mornin',
  (An' true the mornin's ane no tae resist);
Ye're blythe an' ye're bonnie, there's na use denyin',
  An' cheerfu' as though ye were just newly kiss'd."

Young Maggie turned roon, ilka ee beamin' brightly,
  An' glintin' wi' mischief full tae the brim,
She turned up her coquettish, bonnie head lightly,
  An' darted her liquid black ee full at him ;
"Gin ye think, sir," she said, "that a kiss maks ane
    cheerie,
  An' gars ane be blythesome an' merry as this,
Maw donkey ahint there seems drowsy an' lazy,
  Ye'd better just gie the puir beastie a kiss !"

MY FAIRY.

Have you seen my winsome fairy,
  She's a laughing little maid,
And she dwells among the flowers
  Down a bracken-bosky glade ;
Have you met her not at evening
  With an old man hand-in-hand ?
Did her beauty fail to give you
  Glimpses into fairy-land ?

First I met her by a brooklet,
　And she sang a soft refrain,
And the water danced toward her,
　Giving back the same sweet strain ;
While she sang the water listened,
　And it strove to imitate,
And a linnet in the hawthorn
　Tried to pipe it to his mate.

And a lambkin in the pasture
　Gravely listened to her song,
And the hills sent back the echo
　On the breeze that came along ;
And the lambkin heard the echo,
　And he glanced toward the hill,
And his face seemed wondrous puzzled
　As he stood so mute and still.

And she calls that old man "Grand-da,"
　For he loves the darling well ;
So he told me all her story
　As we sauntered down the dell,—
How this loved and lovely maiden,
　With her face so sweet and fair,
Caught a sunbeam in the meshes
　Of her silk-shot golden hair.

How that sunbeam fought and struggled,
　Like a web-entangled fly,
Till it spread around her forehead,
　Till it settled in each eye;
And her liplets watched the struggle
　Till they smiled to see the fun,
And, as if by some enchantment,
　That sweet smile has never gone.

You will meet her in the valley
　Where wild bees flit through the wood,
And those wild bees seem to fancy
　That her mouth's a half-op'd bud;
True! she's only yet a maiden,
　And with me she's sweetly shy,
But I bid my heart await her,
　She'll be a woman by and bye.

Once she's mine, I'll always love her,
　And I'll love her shimm'ring hair;
Though the gold be streaked with silver,
　Yet I'll see the sunbeams there;
And along the flower-starred pastures
　Of our life's sweet path we'll roam,
Till the harvest all is garnered
　And the Master calls us home.

HOME AGAIN.

I hear again the village bells
   Across the water sounding,
The music softly peals and swells,
   And on the waves are bounding ;
The blackbird trills his latent song,
   The breeze is perfume bringing,
And dying, distant woods among,
   Still are the sweet bells ringing.

I see the dear loved cot once more,
   Each beauty pictured clearly,
And every scene I loved before
   I seem to love more dearly ;
I gaze across the daisied mead,
   Where my light steps are wending,
And mark where different pathways lead,
   'Mong elm trees gaunt and bending.

Each dear spot by the river's side,
   ' The water rough and shallow,
The mossy stepstones o'er its tide,
    All seems my thoughts to hallow ;
And as I slowly wander on
    Sweet thrills of pleasure feeling,
Thinking of days for ever gone,
    I hear the church bells pealing.

BY THE ELDER BUSH.

By the elder bush I met her,
    When her face was young and fair,
When the evening odours wandered
    On the soothing Sabbath air.
Down the lane the church bells pealing
    Sent a music through the grove,
And the growing twilight, stealing,
    Lent a sweetness to our love.

By the river's brink we rambled,
  And we whispered nothings sweet
While the wimpling water gambol'd,
  Eddying softly 'neath our feet ;
Up the bankside, 'mong the brackens,
  Sweetly chirp'd a lonely bird,
And the balmy breezes, breathing,
  Through the stunted bushes stirred.

There I told her all my yearning,
  While her hand in mine I press'd,
And my heart with love was burning
  As she leant upon my breast ;
There I vow'd to love her always,
  Swearing I would love no less ;
There I softly put the question,
  And received the answer, " Yes."

TO A LADY.

When naught disturbed my spirit's calm,
   And life's rude strife was hushed awhile,
Bathed in a sweet ethereal balm
   My sorrow's face moved in a smile ;
And in that transient time of bliss
   A spark of hope I dared to see,
Gazing beyond the scenes of this
   I thought of thee ! I thought of thee !

Still when the stream of care ebbs low,
   And the pure air of rest I breathe,
Where the Wear's waters calmly flow,
   Garlands of airy forms I wreathe ;
Yearning to make thee all my own,
   Yet fearing it may never be ;
Longing to make my passion known,
   I think of thee ! I think of thee !

And if my hopes are doomed to die,
   Speak not their doom in dulcet tone,
'Twill only add to every sigh
   Pangs that will make such sigh a groan ;
Yet oh! sweet nymph, be ever sure,
   While living, at thy shrine I'll be ;
And every day and every hour
   I'll think of thee! I'll think of thee !

THE PATH THROUGH THE OLD CHURCHYARD.

Where grey-grown St. Michael's*rears proudly its head,
   Bold outlined and regally grand,
As if in its constancy guarding the dead
   Enclasped in that green plot of land ;
'Tis there is a path which, above all the rest,
   Claims my tenderest, holiest regard ;
A spot of the halo of sanctity blest,
   The path through the old churchyard.

*St. Michael's, the Parish Church, Houghton-le-Spring.

G

On memory's wings, to my fancy's keen eye,
  A scene from the fair past appears,
A bright recollection that never shall die,
  But reign on unchanged through long years ;
It paints to my fancy a picture of youth,
  School-children in crooked file paired,
A two-deep procession, half noisy, half hushed,
  Up that path through the old churchyard.

It brings me fair pictures in bridal array,
  Sweet faces but partly concealed,
Fair pictures of blushes and orange bloom spray,
  That speak of great vows to be sealed ;
It hints of the joys and the trials to come,
  The sun and the gloom to be shared ;
It shows me light feet that keep time to the heart
  Up that path through the old churchyard.

It shows me processions in sable attire,
  So solemn, so silent, and calm,
Some heart-broken mother, some sorrowing sire,
  For whose bleeding heart there's no balm ;
It shows me mute groups of fond, sorrowing friends,
  Bemoaning bereavement so hard ;
It shows me a path, long and crooked, which ends
  In this path through the old churchyard.

At night, when the town's busy traffic is done,
 The bustle and racket grown still,
'Tis pleasant to cull from the years that are gone,
 Those pictures which through the heart thrill ;
And here have I gathered such memories oft,
 While night's smiling monarch held ward,—
And spectre-like, brightly illumined the tombs
 Near the path through the old churchyard.

TELL ME THE STORY AGAIN.

Mother dear ! tell me the story again,
 The story I'm ever so eager to hear,
How in my boyhood I caused you pain,
 And racked your bosom with care and fear ;
The pleasing tale of the drifted days,
 The fairest link in my life's rude chain,
Of the fancied joys of my scapegrace ways,
 Come, tell me the story again.

Well I remember the morals you taught me,
 Honour and honesty, justice and truth,
Yet I'm afraid I was apt to be heedless
 In those wild days of my graceless youth.

Oh ! how I love for to hear you tell
　How my quickly-born hopes were as quickly slain,
How one by one my air-castles fell ;
　Come, tell me the story again.

Oh ! I doubt not I was wayward and wild,
　Wilful and wayward and hard to bend ;
But those crooked ways of a heedless child
　Will straighten, in manhood, to one great end,
The love of the dear old parent stem
　That nourished the bud through wind and rain ;
Yet, oh ! what a flood of wild fancy is raised
　To hear the old story again.

YEARS AGO.

'Twas thus we beguiled the invisible hours,
　　Long ago ! long ago !
Culling the rarest and choicest flowers
　That bared their hearts to the sun's warm glow;
Down where the roses grew thick on the wall,
By the air-cooling fountain's tingling fall,
　　Years and years ago !

In the sun-gilded hours of our early love,
  Long ago ! long ago !
Our hearts were as pure as the air above,
 As tender and soft as the turf below ;
In the arbour, where, down o'er the doorway swung
The creepers that fast to the trellis-work clung,
  Years and years ago !

In the years ago when we plighted our troth,
  Long ago ! long ago !
We vow'd to be trustful and constant both,
 And to love each other come weal or woe :
And constant we've been from that moment of bliss,
When we sealed our pledge with a ling'ring kiss,
  Years and years ago !

In the time to come we will think of the past,
  Long ago ! long ago !
Of the day when together our lots we cast,
 Down the path where the Tiesa's waters flow ;
And, dwelling together, we'll still defy
The troubles we scorned in the days gone by,
  Years and years ago !

ONLY A CARTE-DE-VISITE.

Only a carte-de-visite !
But oh ! such a dear little baby face,
Where the clouds and smiles each other chase,
    And the lips are, oh ! so sweet !

Only a carte-de-visite !
A plump little form on a high-back'd chair,
A round little head with curly hair
    And motionless, slippered feet.

Only a carte-de-visite !
A face with such dear little merry eyes
That dance, or in turn look full of surprise,
    And a dimpled chin so neat.

Only a mute photograph !
Yet oh ! such a sweet little baby face
Around whose mouth you can almost trace
    An inclination to laugh.

HOME.

Home, to the youth, is where a mother
   Tends upon his every ill ;
Where a sister, or a brother,
   Helps him up life's toilsome hill ;
Where the dear familiar objects
   Seem a part of life to him ;
To be robbed of these attractions
   Makes the youth's existence dim.

Home, to the man, is where the dear one,
   Whom he took to be his wife,
Waits at night with kindly cheer, on
   His return from labour's strife ;
Where the lisping, blue-eyed darling
   Coos a welcome sweet to him ;
To be robbed of these attractions
   Makes the man's existence dim.

Home, to the wife, is where the husband
   Cheers the hearth with smiles and songs,
Where he watches o'er the household,
   Making rights and smoothing wrongs ;

And, while he bestows attentions,
   She would move a world for him ;
To be robbed of love's attractions
   Makes the wife's existence dim.

Home, to the aged, when life's weary,
   Where? oh ! where can they find home ?
When the world is bleak and dreary,
   Home must lie beyond the tomb ;
What unphilosophic mortal
   Feels there's no new state for him?
Tell the old they've no hereafter,
   And you make their last hours dim.

A HARVEST NIGHT.

Soft September tints the barley
   With the glow of pale moonlight,
And the breath that scarce gives motion
   Steals upon the wings of night ;
And the harvest perfumes wander
   Through the wood and o'er the heath,
While night's monarch in his grandeur
   Smiles on golden plains beneath.

In the solemn hush I wander,
  Tempted by the balmy night,
And my spirit breathes its rapture
  In soft sighs of sweet delight ;
And the sleepy breeze, arousing,
  Gently stirs the fallen leaves,
And he laughs and seems to tell me
  How he kissed the golden sheaves.

Then, in playful circles sporting,
  Throws a dead leaf at my feet,
And he whispers all his flirting
  With the patch of blushing wheat.
Then he hurries down the valley,
  Breathing odours as he goes,
Skimming down the tingling brooklet
  That beneath the hawthorn flows.

Waving fields, already golden,
  Smile back at the moonbeams bold,
Till a passing cloud between them
  Sweeps its shadow down the gold ;
And the uncut stretch of beauty
  Bends its head so fair and bright,
Doing homage to the monarch
  Of this lovely harvest night.

"HER FACE WAS HER FORTUNE."

Fondly I cherish the olden-time memory,
    Still do I think of the days that are gone,
Oft-times recalling the tender endearments,
    Although the dim past has long hurried them on;
Vividly now soft remembrance is bringing
    Clear recollections of moments gone by,
And to my heart-strings are faithfully clinging
    Thoughts of the days when my Norah was nigh;
            For her face was her fortune,
                Oh, such a fortune!
        And we were happy, my Norah and I.

Wealthy she was, but her wealth was her beauty;
    Liquid her eyes were, and dancing with love;
Rich in her voice, which was mellow and fluty,
    And smote me like breathings from regions above;
Clearly still does remembrance come o'er me,
    And I remember the love-lighted eye;
Scenes of the past ever flitting before me,
    Bring back the thoughts of when Norah was nigh;
            For her face was her fortune,
                Oh, such a fortune!
        And we were constant, my Norah and I.

Yet, while I'm thinking, the shadows beset me,
   And I remember too well how she died ;
Loving till death, as she was when she met me,
   Oh, I was robbed of my beautiful bride.
Though she was poor yet I cherished her fondly,
   Now o'er her memory in sadness I sigh ;
In the fair gilt of the days that are drifted,
   Naught else I cared for when Norah was nigh :
      For her face was her fortune,
      Oh, such a fortune !
And we were happy, my Norah and I.

THE LITTLE PINK LETTER.

Expectant she stands at the window,
   And eagerly glances around,
With eyes beaming liquid and tender
   She starts at the slightest foot-sound ;
Wishful, and impatiently longing,
   Thinking of first this and then that,
Pictures her memory thronging,
   At last comes the postman's rat tat.

She bounds to the door, and, oh Cupid !
    An envelope perfumed and pink !
That postman so rude and so stupid
    Is laughing, oh ! what will he think ?
He guesses the cause of her hurry,
    And smiles as she opens the door ;
Sure, a man so unseemingly merry
    Ne'er brought a love-letter before !

Sly glancing, he hands her the treasure,
    With many a " hem " and a quiz,
And, struggling to hide her own pleasure,
    She thinks what a slow man he is.
At last, the frail note firmly clasping,
    With delight ne'er experienced before,
And her skirts in her hand firmly grasping,
    She darts in and clashes the door.

And now, in the strictest seclusion,
    Her heart pants, and how her cheeks burn
As, opening it free from intrusion,
    She reads it and kisses by turn ;
From where it commences, " My darling !"
    And runs on in rapturous strain,
Right down to the words, "Till death parts us,"
    She kisses and reads it again.

WILL YOU BE WILLING.

Down where the sunset is tinting the meadows,
  Down where the brooklets so gushingly sing,
In still hours of evening we'll wander together,
  And list to the bells as they merrily ring ;
You shall have more than the brooklets to cheer you,
  You shall have words of affection, my dear,
None save myself and the birdlings shall hear you,
  I have a sweet tale of love for your ear :
      But tell me, my darling,
Will you the name of your parents resign ?
      In time that's to come
      Will you come to my home?
Will you be willing, my sweet, to be mine ?

Will you be willing to brighten my hearthstone ?
  Will you be willing to tend to my board ?
Will you be willing to govern my household,
  Where all the things I hold dearest are stored ?

Will you be willing to smile when I'm joyous?
  Will you be willing to weep when I mourn?
Will you be willing to tend me in sickness,
  And comfort me when I am sad-and forlorn?
      Oh ! tell me, my darling,
Shall your sweet face ever near me shine?
      In time that's to come
      Will you come to my home ?
Will you be willing, my sweet, to be mine ?

Will you not give your fond care and sweet comfort
  To the silver-haired woman who gave me my birth ?
Will you be willing to soothe her last moments
  And sweeten her path from this troublesome earth?
Will you be willing to gather life's flowers
  And strew them in freshness around her path ?
Will you be willing to lend her your sunshine
  And brighten the few years remaining she hath ?
      And tell me, my darling,
Will you not bid my heart cease to repine ?
      In time that's to come
      Will you come to my home ?
Will you be willing, my sweet, to be mine ?

PLEASURES ARE TRANSIENT.

A blackbird sang in the hawthorn hedge,
    And I listened, enthralled by his song,
And I said, "Sweet songster, tarry awhile,
    And your silvery strains prolong."
But the sweet song ceased, and away he fled,
    And all was hushed again,
My heart again sunk sad and dead
    And the pleasure burst in pain.

A brook ran by with its music sweet,
    And it sang me a murmuring song,
And I said, as it hurried below my feet,
    "Sweet brooklet, thy stay prolong;"
But it only babbled a murmur low
    And went on its seaward march,
And methought its music died in a moan
    As it dashed beneath an arch.

BEAUTIFUL THROSTLE.

Beautiful throstle, that warbled so sweetly,
   Dull is the winter unblest by thy song,
And my heart, saddened, is mourning and waiting,
   Waiting to hear thee with yearnings so strong ;
Bird of the silver song, come with the summer,
   Come when the daisies bespangle the lea,
And when the woodlands with songs are redolent,
   Beautiful throstle, come whistle to me !
         Beautiful bird !
         Beautiful bird !
   Come into the willow and sing to me.

There's a sweet grot not far down in the garden,
   Roses down there in the summer will grow,
And a tall willow bends over the arbour,
   Though now its branches are covered with snow ;
Come in the summer, and there in the arbour
   I'll listen enraptured, my soul roaming free ;
I'll tune my sad lyre to the song thou art singing,
   Beautiful throstle, come whistle to me !
     .   Beautiful bird !
         Beautiful bird !
   Come into the willow and sing to me.

DEAD.

When the linnet, that sang in the willow last Summer,
  Ceased singing, and fled to some far-distant grove,
The light of my bosom was darkened and vanished,
  My heart suffered loss in the death of its love.
Through long dreary weeks she lay propped on her
      pillow,
  Till sorrow's dark night broke in silvery day ;
One evening she sank as the sun was just setting,
  "The pearl of great price" left the casket of clay.

Ah ! dearly she loved that sweet song of the linnet,
  Trilled from the green willow that tapped on the
      pane,
And softly she spoke of the hope he breathed in it,
  Of her hearing soon a more wonderful strain.
Up over the garden sweet perfumes came floating,
  And borne through the casement they scented the
      room ;
And faintly she murmured of perfumes far sweeter
  Away in the light, somewhere out of life's gloom.

H

At last came the end, over Styx's gloomy billow
   She sailed to the sweet spirit-land of the dead ;
They carved on her tombstone an urn and a willow,
   And planted sweet violets over her bed ;
And now the sweet birds and the bees hover near her,
   A linnet perchance sings among the long grass,
The perfumes sail softly and lovingly round her,
   The winds hush their voices and sigh as they pass.

Ah ! fondly we trusted and hoped for the future,
   What visions we saw, and what pictures we limn'd,
And out of the past we extracted the sunshine,
   At last came the gloom, and the brightness was
      dim'd.
And often I roam when the night shadows gather,
   And daytime's rude mock'ry of glitter is fled,
And here by the mound where my heart's light is
      sleeping,
   I breathe out my spirit in prayer for the dead.

THE ORPHAN'S WAIL.

The wind went whistling over the stones,
And chilled the homeless mendicant's bones,
And bore on each gust the pitiful groans
 Of the wailing one out in the night :
  And the wind was wild,
  And an orphan child
 Lay crouching, a pitiful sight.

The snow-covered travellers went coolly by,
And seemed not to care for the orphan's cry,
"Help, help me for pity ! I faint, I die !"
 And the lonely one out in the street
  Still shudder'd and cried,
  Still struggled to hide
 The swollen and bleeding feet.

He lay on a doorstep benumbed with cold,
And oh ! what a sorrowful tale he told,
While the man of the house rolled in his gold,
 That weary one, out in the street,
  Lay crouching there
  In the biting air,
 And craved for something to eat.

The hair was dishevel'd, the hands were blue,
And the lone one cried, as the snowflakes flew,
"Give me bread, I am cold and hungry too,
    I'm dying out here in the street;
        For the cold winds blow,
        I've nowhere to go,
    Oh! give me something to eat!"

"Oh, Father of heaven! look down on me,
I've no one to pity me now but Thee,
Oh, set my poor slumbering spirit free,
    And take my soul out of the street,
        Up, up through the sky
        To Thy throne on high,
    To dwell with the angels sweet!"

The Father heard, and He quickly replied
To the orphan boy as he wildly cried;
And, before the grey morning broke, he died,
    Out, out in that fearful night,
        The morning broke mild
        On the orphan child,
    But the soul had taken its flight.

REST AWHILE.

Hush ! oh, hush ! the clang of traffic !
  See ! the woods are robed in brown ;
Rest, ye busy worldly workers,
  Look ! the leaves are dropping down ;
Summer's fled and Autumn's flying,
  Soon the birds will hush their strains,
Now the beauties all are dying,
  And across the leaf-strewn plains
Comes the voice of chanting Autumn,
  Mournfully o'er hill and vale ;
Hush ! oh, hush ! the clang of traffic,
  Let us hear her dying wail.

Hush your noise for one brief hour,
  Listen to the last sweet song,
Soon all nature will be buried
  In a winter drear and long ;
From the Autumn woodland, gushing,
  Comes a chorus sweetly clear,

And the sighing zephyrs, rushing,
   Call on all to rest and hear;
This may be the last great chorus,
   Hush! and hear the sweet refrain;
Hear the woods sob down to slumber,
   Then go back to life again.

THE BROOK'S DILEMMA.

There's a grot beneath the brambles,
   In the wood's secluded nook,
Where the trailing ivy scrambles
   Up the bank side near the brook;
And the water, southward flowing,
   Tells the story of its love,
With its silver bosom glowing,
   To the flowers that bloom above.

There a primrose, golden-breasted,
   Blushed to hear the brooklet's song,
And with violet she jested,
   Who had loved the water long;

And, before the spring-tide vanish'd,
　　Serious grew the jealous jest,
For both violet and primrose
　　Wondered which the brook loved best.

"Ah!" I heard the water murmur,
　　As he purled and wimpled on,
"I have sung the Spring to Summer,
　　And my flowers are dead and gone,
Yet which of them looked the neatest
　　Always puzzled me to tell,
And I know not which was sweetest,
　　For I loved them both so well."

A SONG FOR SPRING.

Oh! have you not heard the blackbird's sweet note,
　　Down there in the tall chesnut tree?
And have you not caught the perfumes, as they float
　　Song-laden over the lea?
And did you not see a white butterfly pass
　　And flit o'er the garden hedge?
And have you not heard the brook's gurgling voice
　　As it wanders away through the sedge?

Oh ! listen, the blackbird is singing again,
   How sweet and how clear is his voice !
Look ! there is a butterfly down in the lane,
   How everything seems to rejoice !
The fields will be yellow with cowslips ere long,
   And Nature her tribute will bring
To welcome again the sweet season of song,
   The beautiful, beautiful Spring !

BLUE IN THE SKY.

So long as there's blue in the sky of my life
   I'll laugh at the threatening clouds,
In songs I will smother the racket of strife,
   And struggle to fold back the shrouds ;
I'll keep up the music and sing to the strain
   If my love is but lingering nigh,
And I'll hope for the sunshine and brightness again,
   So long as there's blue in the sky.

So long as there's only a streak or a speck
   I'll peer through the cloven gloom,
And the uprising dread I will struggle to check
   And smile when the thunders shall boom ;

I'll look through the showers and hope for the best
    And in time the dark shadows will fly,
And not for one hour shall my mind be distrest
    So long as there's blue in the sky.

There's hope if there's only a glimmer of light,
    And, hopeful, I'm waiting the dawn ;
My Father will watch through the murk of the night,
    And clarion the breaking of morn ;
The sun may yet smile through the ocean of tears,
    Then why should my soul droop and die ?
Be calm, oh ! my bosom, and stifle thy fears,
    There's blue in thy life's clouded sky !

OUT OF THE PAST.

When the south wind softly wandered
    Down the maple-skirted grove,
There I sauntered with my Zilla,
    And we laughed and talked of love ;
And the passing breezes, sporting
    With the tangles of her hair,
Went and whispered all our flirting
    To a brook that gurgled there.

When I stooped and softly kissed her
  On the lips I loved so well,
Wanton breezes caught the echo
  And they laughed it down the dell;
Arm in arm we slowly rambled,
  And we kissed and sang by turns,
Watching rabbits as they gambol'd
  'Mong the briars, whins, and ferns.

How she sigh'd when I retold her
  That sweet tale I'd told her oft;
Though oft told it seemed no older,
  For the blush-tint, rich and soft,—
Added to her cheeks new beauty
  As she looked me in the eyes,
And the vows she would have spoken
  Lost themselves in smiles and sighs.

Well, we're growing old together,
  And though Time, with rough-shod feet,
Brings us fits of stormy weather,
  Yet to-day her smiles are sweet;
And we sometimes talk it over,
  How the golden hours we spent,
When the odour of the clover
  Blended with the woodbine's scent.

Ah! we've lived a life of sunshine,
  And we trust we've done our best
To send down some gleams of brightness
  Into some poor toiler's breast;
And before the lowering curtain
  Of this life is all unfurled,
We expect to leave some foot-tracks
  On the highway of the world.

THE BRIGHT SIDE.

Mine! all my own, through the long years to come,
  Partner of all my trials and joys,
Star of my hitherto lightless home,
  Now can I laugh at life's jangle and noise!
For there's a music amidst it all
  Like to my dreams of the after-heaven;
And there's a hush in the midst of the squall,
  Nursing the bark that has been tempest-driven.
        Pulse of my heart!
        Till death shall us part
We'll drink of the nectar that love has given!

What shall we say to the troubles we meet?
   Shall we not smile, and look calmly on?
Shall we not gather the flowers at our feet
   And smile as we bid all the shadows begone?
What tho' the rain comes damping down
   And scatters the leaves of our full-blown flower,
Have we not plenty of buds partly blown
   To come out more fresh from the harmless shower?
        Pulse of my heart!
        Till death shall us part
We'll gather the blossoms of every hour!

Treasures of love that no man can count,
   Cottage-love life of the purest gold,
These will the greatest of sorrows surmount
   If we but tread with feet steady and bold;
Perish the thought of a burden too great!
   Laugh at the dream of a looming cloud!
We'll hold out our arms to the favours of fate,
   And bury all ills in oblivion's shroud.
        Pulse of my heart!
        Till death shall us part
We'll toil up the hill and keep laughing aloud!

CALLED AWAY.

Through an open chamber window,
   Borne upon the silent air,
Came a voice so low and tender,
   'Mid a wail of sad despair.

" I am dying, dearest, dying,
   All the joys of life are past;
Dry your eyes and cease your crying,
   You're my first love and my last !

" Let this consolation bear you
   Through the weary world of strife ;
Yet I would not it should mar you
   From a future married life.

" Only this last painful parting
   Binds me to the world I leave,
When for home my soul is starting
   Why then should my darling grieve ?

" Yes ! I know 'tis sad to lose me,
   Life and love to all are sweet,
'Twas decreed that you should choose me
   ` From the many at your feet !

"Come then, kiss me, darling, kiss me!
    Let your heart be strong and brave;
You, I know, are sure to miss me,
    But we'll meet beyond the grave!"

Then their lips were locked together
    In the last warm kiss of love;
Then their loving souls were parted;
    Her's below and his above.

———————

WHEN WE WERE CHILDREN TOGETHER.

Do you remember how sweetly we prattled
    When we were children together, my love,
Culling, in shelter, the white petal'd daisies
    Where the great elm tree stood towering above?
Do you remember the stories I told you,
    'Neath the trees in that soft summer weather?
You struggled to go, and I struggled to hold you,
        When we were children together;
When we were children together, my sweet,
And the flowers beguiled our wandering feet,
        When we were children together.

Do you remember the path through the meadows,
  Where oft we rambled together, my love?
Lest we might startle the lark from her cover,
  We thought it a pity to speak or move.
Do you remember the butterfly chasing
  Knee-deep in the sweet purple heather?
How down the hill-side we went merrily racing,
    When we were children together?
When we were children together, my sweet,
And far from our homes strayed our wand'ring feet,
    When we were children together.

Do you remember the clustering brambles,
  When we were children together, my love,
The berries we picked in our afternoon rambles?
  You waited below while I clambered above.
Do you know when we homeward went merrily tripping
  In the hush of that calm summer weather,
How down the green lane we went cheerfully skipping,
    When we were children together?
When we were children together, my sweet,
And homeward went tripping our toddling feet,
    When we were children together.

JANUARY.

Dim bursts the dawn of January morn,
 The city's smoke salutes the chilly day;
White, snow-capped hills, the face of earth adorn,
 And wildly sweeps the wind away, away!
   The bare gaunt trees
   Wave in the breeze,
And o'er the sky in one great stream,
 Clouds, black and white, together run,
With now and then a fitful gleam
   Of silver sun.

Hard on December's track he madly tears,
 Cold, wild, and bleak, grim January grey;
On his grim forehead cheerless frowns he bears,
 And wildly sweeps the wind away, away!
   The bare gaunt trees
   Wave in the breeze;
And, with the semblance of a dream,
 The clouds sweep past the fitful sight,
And, separating, show a gleam
   Of liquid light.

WOO'D, WEDDED, AND WIDOW'D.

The sun came up over the hill
And smiled on the leaflets brown and sear,
And told the frost-rind its doom was near;
He scared the gloom into the wood's deep nook,
And blinked in the face of the quivering brook;
The lovely morn blushed as she felt the first throe
Of a love that was making her bosom glow,
    When the sun came up over the hill.

The sun lit the beautiful grove:
The morning reclined on the daisied earth,
As out of the mist-land he sallied forth,
Her fair roseate cheeks with joy were flushed,
The brighter he smiled the more she blushed;
He stole down the mountain and kissed her eyes,
And in zephyrs she breathed her answering sighs
    To the tale of his passionate love.

I

The morn drank the sun's sweet words :
And, ere the long hours could all be gone,
The souls of the lovers were blended in one ;
He woo'd her with smiles so sweetly bright,
Her heart met his in a wild delight ;
The rills and the waterfalls tingled in tune,
And the morn and the sunlight were wedded at noon,
    And their nuptials were sung by the birds.

    The dial told Time's rapid flight,
And slowly the sun wandered down to his rest,
And a gloom settled over the day's soft breast ;
The bridegroom sunk from the arc above,
And the day wept rain when she lost her love ;
In silence she sorrow'd, nor ever a word
Of complaint left her lips as she followed her lord,
    And sunk into sad-visaged night.

HIS ONE EWE LAMB.

They lived in a hut on the skirt of a wood,
  A grey-haired old man and a maiden,
And down by the door sang the river's cold flood,
  'Twixt banks that with wild flowers were laden ;
A grand-child she was, and he loved her so well,
  She bore such a sweetness about her ;
And oft, to the stranger, in rapture he'd tell
  How life would be dreary without her.

One day came a lordling, attractive and gay,
  With smiles most delusive and winning ;
And ah ! when he first saw the beautiful fay,
  He woo'd her, and won in beginning ;
She trusted, he triumphed, betrayed her and fled,
  Entranced by the eyes of another ;
Months passed, and that hut held two forms cold
        and dead,
  A newly-born babe and its mother.

One day went a solemn cortege down the lane,
    The trees mourned as soft breezes stirred them,
And sad were the looks and keen was the pain
    As they under the willows interred them;
That night the betrayer by chance wandered past,
    And saw that which made his heart shiver,—
A grey-bearded face cold and dead, upward cast,
    Among the long flags in the river.

———————

A SHADOW CAST BEFORE.

Mother, I sat in the meadow to-day,
Sat in the meadow and wove me a garland,
    And, among buttercups yellow and gay,
    Fastened fair flowers and hawthorn spray;
Daisies more bright than yon gems in the starland,
    Hawthorn as fair as the sweet face of May;
Wove them together and made me a garland,
      Wove me a garland so gay.

Mother, I gathered the flowers so fair,
Gathered them all in their freshness and sweetness ;
  Warm was the sunshine and sweet was the air
  As I arranged them and bound them with care,
Held them at arm's length, admiring their neatness ;
  And I knew not, as I toyed with them there,
How they were losing their freshness and sweetness,
     Losing it all on the air.

Mother, I've brought my dead garland to you,
Brought my dead garland all faded and battered ;
  Once they were brilliant and lovely, 'tis true ;
  Ah ! had I let them remain where they grew,
Now they had not been so jaded and scattered ;
  Thus they would teach me a lesson I knew :
" Child, thus are life's hopes oft faded and battered,
     Faded and battered 'tis true."

REBUKED.

The clouds had dulled from gold to purple deep,
   And stealing o'er the meadlands came the night;
Anon the pale faint stars began to peep
   From heaven's blue arc, as daylight took to flight.
There came soft breathings from the dusky vast,
   Low, measured sighings of the yew-fringed wood.
Down where the bright young moon faint silver cast
   Through the barred wicket gate, a poet stood.

Ah! 'twas a lovely night, the rippled brook
   Wand'ring in vesper murmurs down the vale,
Reflected back to heaven the moon's proud look,
   And mirror'd deep the stars in myriads pale;
"Ah!" sang the brook, "yon countless worlds above
   Grow vain to see their beauty limn'd in me,
)·s of bright globes which in their circle move,
     ing the woods, the vales, the moors, the sea.

" Down in my waters I reflect their light,
    Full-formed and beautiful, Dame Nature's glass
To picture back to heaven the image bright
    Of yonder wandering spheres that nightly pass."
" Hush !" checked a passing breeze that lull'd the
            night,
    " Near by a poet stands and scans the skies,
And every orb now circling through heaven's height
    Is mirror'd in that poet's heart and eyes."

THE AUTHOR'S APOLOGY.

My first little volume is at the bar of public opinion. In the toiling workshop of life I forged these links; amid the toil and bustle, the jangle and noise, I sent out on the world my little effusions. Many of them are known. Should they be accepted, I will venture another volume on your notice. With the hope of success I place under your critical glass

> *These children of an idle brain,*
> *Begot of nothing but vain fantasy,*
> *Which is as thin of substance as the air,*
> *And more inconstant than the wind.*

JOHN ROWELL WALLER.

Houghton-le-Spring,
March, 1878.

www.ingramcontent.com/pod-product-compliance
Lightning Source LLC
Chambersburg PA
CBHW032012010726
47493CB00007B/2363